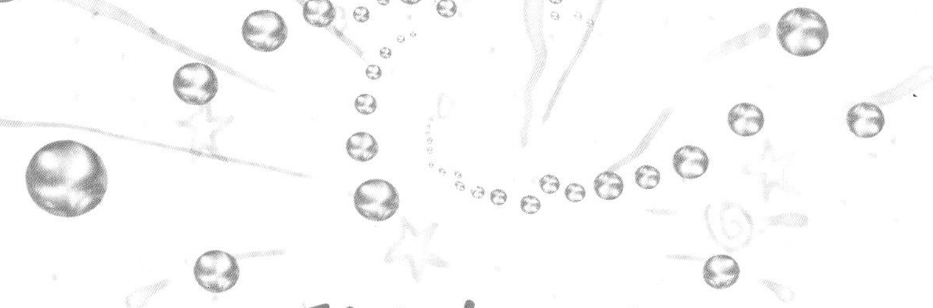

This book belongs to:

.................................................

Oddies Limited, Maritime House, Grafton Square, London, SW4 0JW
www.oddieworld.com



A CIP catalogue record for this book is available from the British Library.

First Published in Great Britain in 2004 by Oddies Limited.

ISBN 1-904745-15-6

Printed in Great Britain

# Nurse Oddie

To Anna

Grant Slatter

The nurse put her favourite pair of socks into the washing machine. She added some washing powder and shut the door.

"Chug-chug, whirr, chug-chug, whirr," went the washing machine. Then it did something strange.

It spun extra fast and all the bubbles bounced around wildly. The machine ballooned. Then there was a supersonic WHOOSH as one of the socks disappeared.

The sock was called Nurse Oddie and she was zooming through space towards Oddieworld. "I expect an Oddie is feeling poorly in Oddieworld," she said.

Nurse Oddie floated down into Oddieworld and popped out of her bubble. “Litterbug Oddie has a strange tummyache,” said a soft voice behind her.

It was Sock Fairy. "You'll find her in that house over there," she said. Nurse Oddie looked round at the house but when she turned back Sock Fairy had disappeared.

A shiny new nurse's watch had appeared in her place. "What a lovely gift!" said Nurse Oddie. "Looks like I am going to have a nice *time* here."

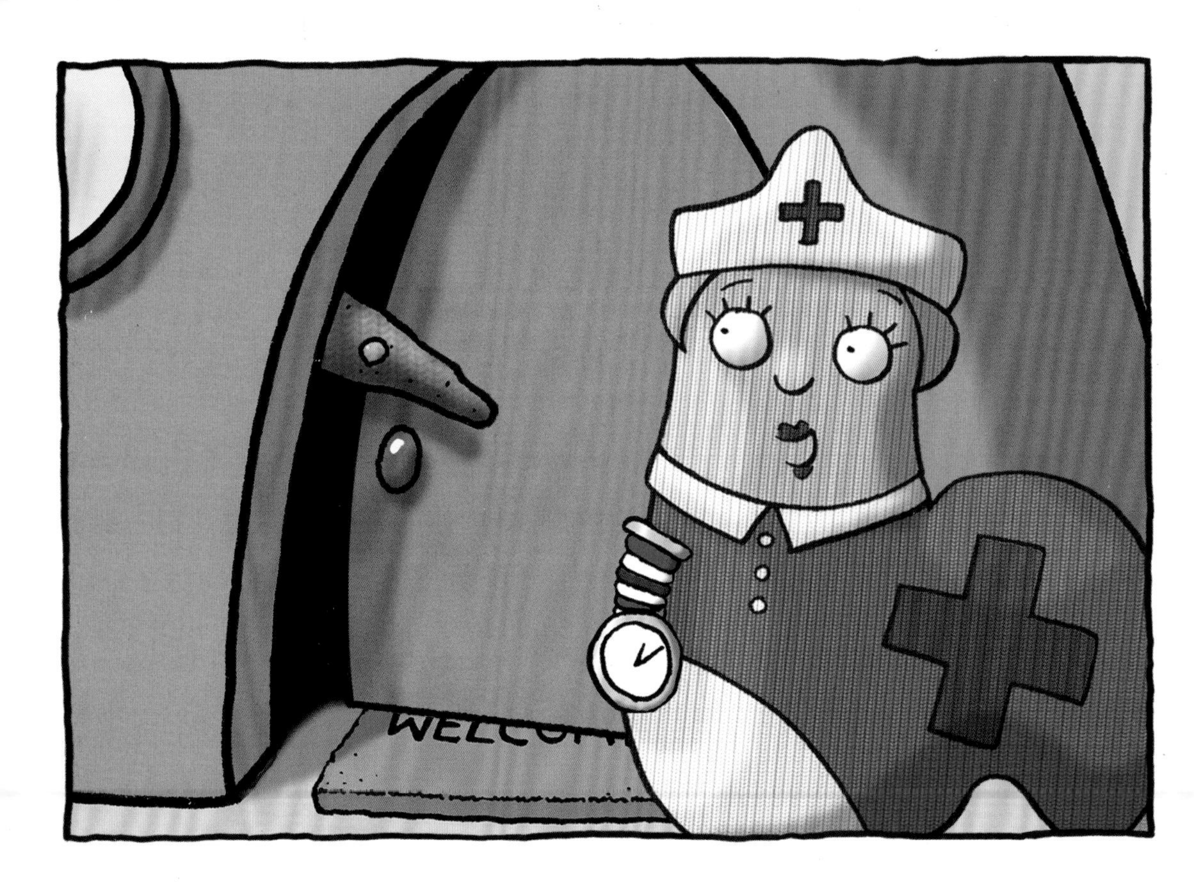

Nurse Oddie knocked on the door of the house. The door opened and a long nose poked out. "Yes?" said the nose. "Oh dear," said Nurse Oddie. "You're not very well at all."

The door flew open. It was Witchy!
"I'm in perfectly bad health," she said. "Now, out of my way. I'm going to give this bag to someone useful."

Nurse Oddie went inside and met Princess Oddie. "Witchy sent Litterbug Oddie over here with a bag of litter but she's not feeling well," said Princess Oddie.

"I brought my favourite pictures of the crown jewels to make her feel better," added Princess Oddie. "They certainly made Witchy smile - she went off all excited."

Nurse Oddie looked at Litterbug.

Then there was a knock at the door.

"I know a spell that can make anyone better," said the voice at the door.
"Thank you, but this is *my* patient," said Nurse Oddie.

Then they heard some strange mutterings outside followed by a big bang. "I think I know who was at the door," said Princess Oddie.

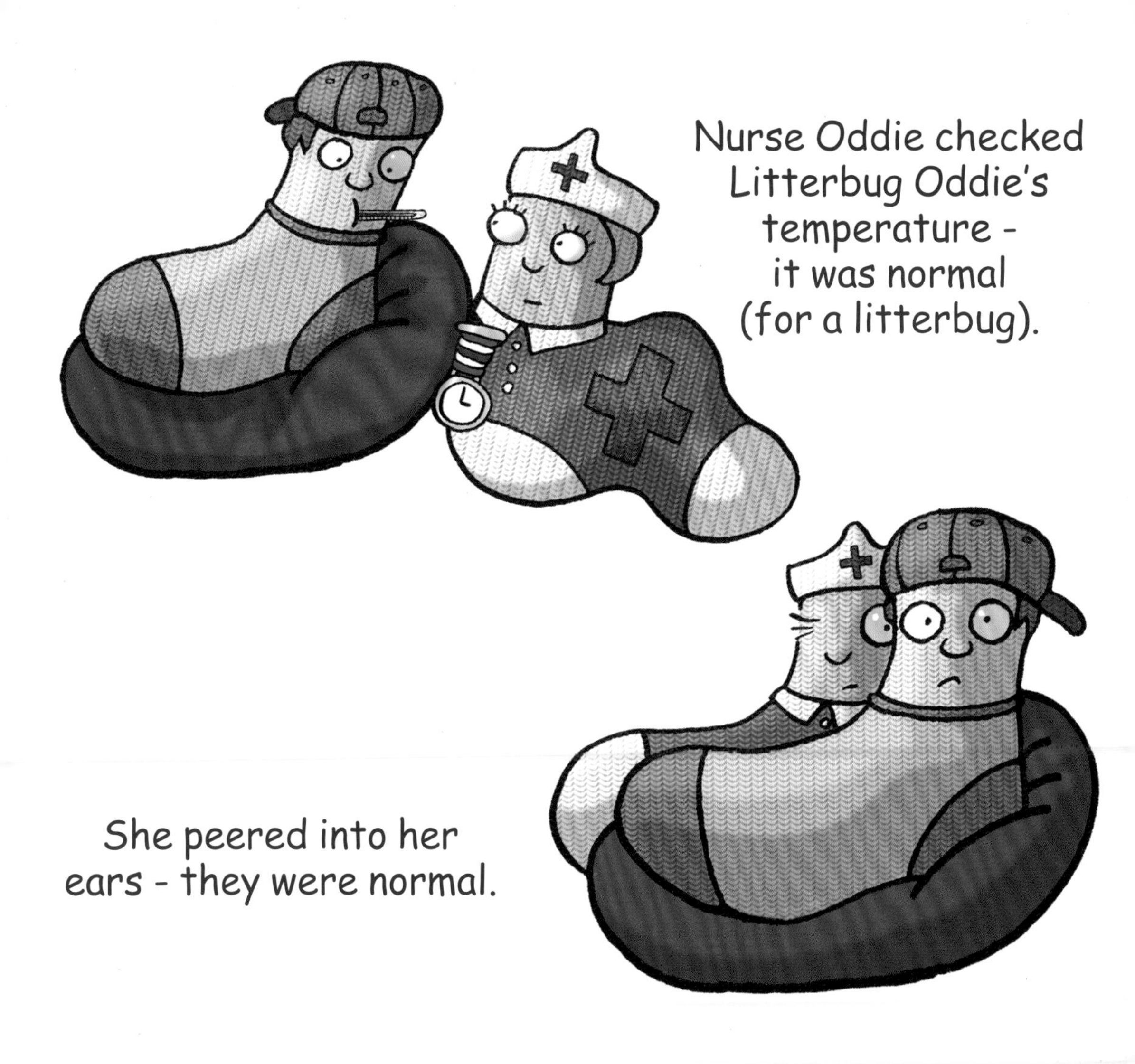

Nurse Oddie checked Litterbug Oddie's temperature - it was normal (for a litterbug).

She peered into her ears - they were normal.

She looked down her throat - it was normal.
Then she listened to her heartbeat - but it was *not* normal.

BICK-BOCK, BICK-BOCK, BICK-BOCK... "That's a strange heartbeat," said Nurse. "Although the sound does remind me of something." Then she heard another sound.

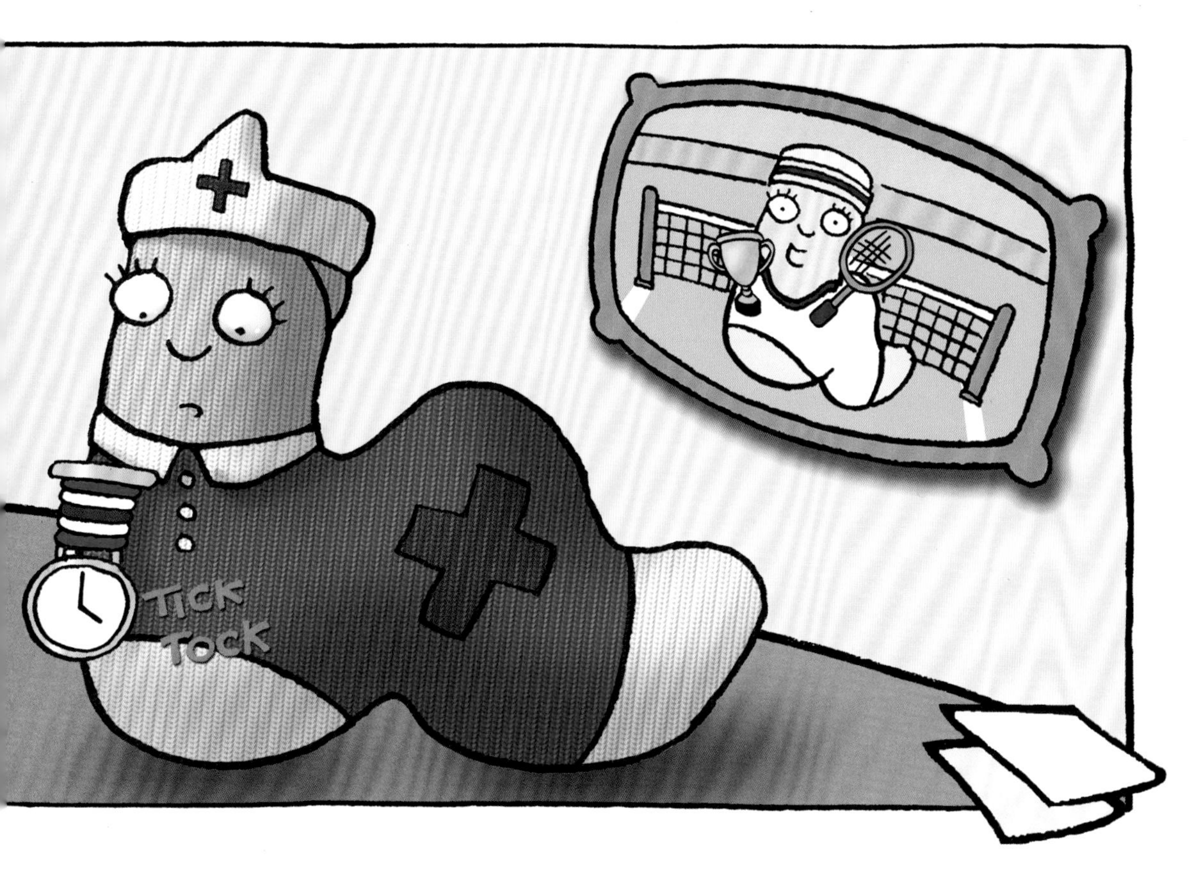


TICK-TOCK, TICK-TOCK, TICK-TOCK... it was her nurse's watch. "Aha!" said Nurse Oddie, "I think we need an X-ray. Let's go to the hospital."

"Just what I thought," said Nurse Oddie.
"You've got a watch inside you!"

"Don't worry," said Surgeon Oddie with a smile. "We'll have that out in no *time*!"

As they came out they saw Wizzo.
"That's my watch," he said. "I was wondering where it had gone."

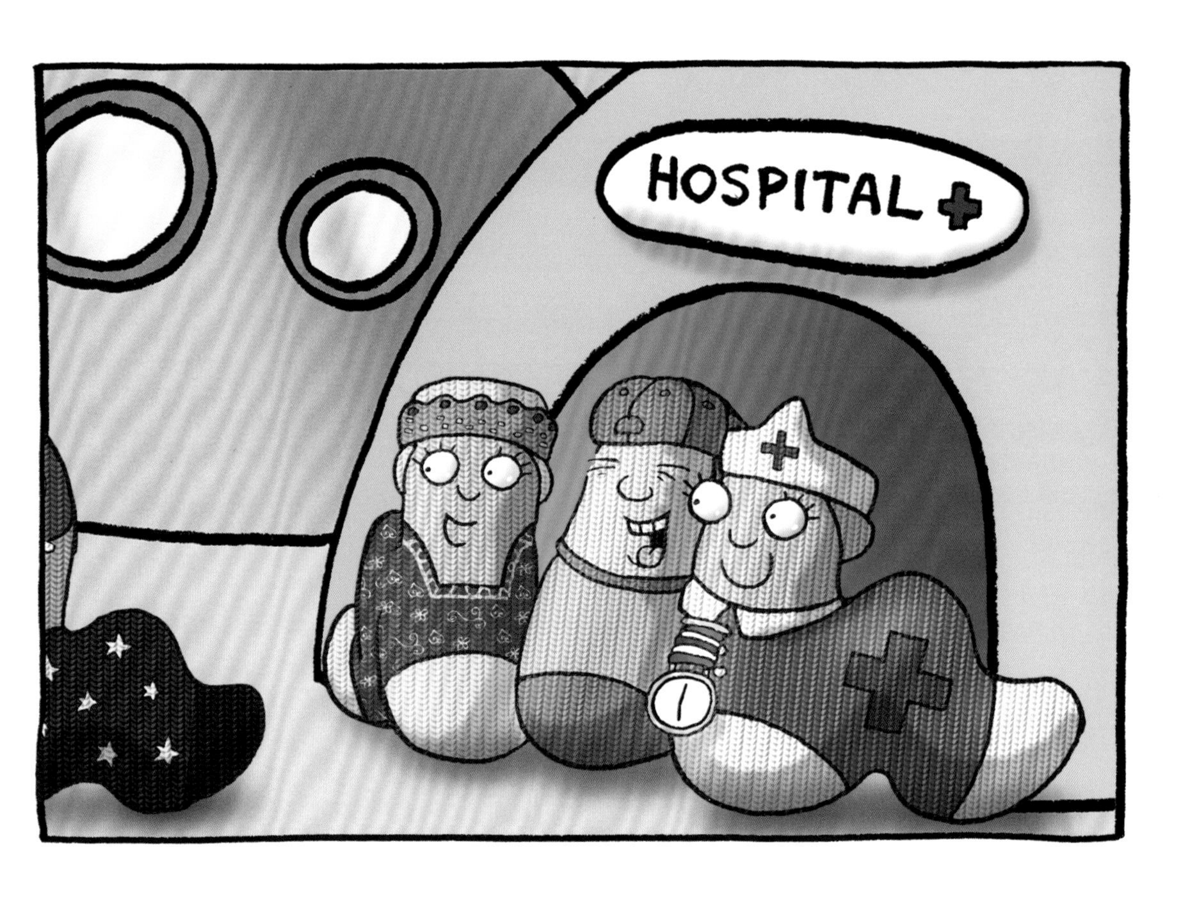


"We'll all *watch* out for your next spell," said Princess Oddie. Everyone giggled.
"Well done Nurse Oddie," said a familiar voice.

It was Sock Fairy. "We'd love you to stay in Oddieworld forever," she said, "but I'll magic you back if that's what you'd really like."

"Well, I think you may need help making other Oddies better," said Nurse Oddie.
"So I'll stay."

Later on Nurse Oddie went to pick some fruit from the trees in Oddie Orchard. She made an Oddelicious Fruit Salad.

"Fruit makes us fit and healthy," said Nurse Oddie. "And, I won't have to use up all my bubble-power making everyone better."

Litterbug Oddie tried some of the fresh fruit. She didn't like to tell the others that it tasted lovely!

Back home, the nurse looked everywhere for her missing sock.

As she snuggled up in bed she asked herself...

"Where do those odd socks go?"

# Have you got the complete collection?

*Nurse Oddie* is the fifth book in the Oddies series. Read the stories of all the other Oddies and their adventures in Oddieworld.

The signposts on Good Oddie Island are all muddled up so Sock Fairy sends for **Police Oddie** - but he soon needs to call for help himself!

The secret is out, odd socks go to Oddieworld! Find out how Oddieworld was formed and how **Wizzo**, **Witchy** and **Sock Fairy** became stuck there.

Good Oddie River has dried up so Sock Fairy sends for **Rugby Oddie** - but only good teamwork can solve this problem.

Witchy wants the Oddie Crown Jewels and calls **Robber Oddie** to help her get them - but he soon learns that crime doesn't pay.

Witchy is cooking up a storm in Oddieworld and Sock Fairy needs some help from **Footy Oddie** - but can he find a way to stop the rain?

# Every Oddie has a story to tell!

## There are lots of games to play plus one secret game!

Find it and complete it and we'll send you a **FREE Oddies poster!**

Be quick and you can win one of the last, original artwork, Oddies posters like this one.

# www.oddieworld.com

**Please Note:** Use of this website may permanently IMPROVE your child's hand/eye co-ordination and intelligence!

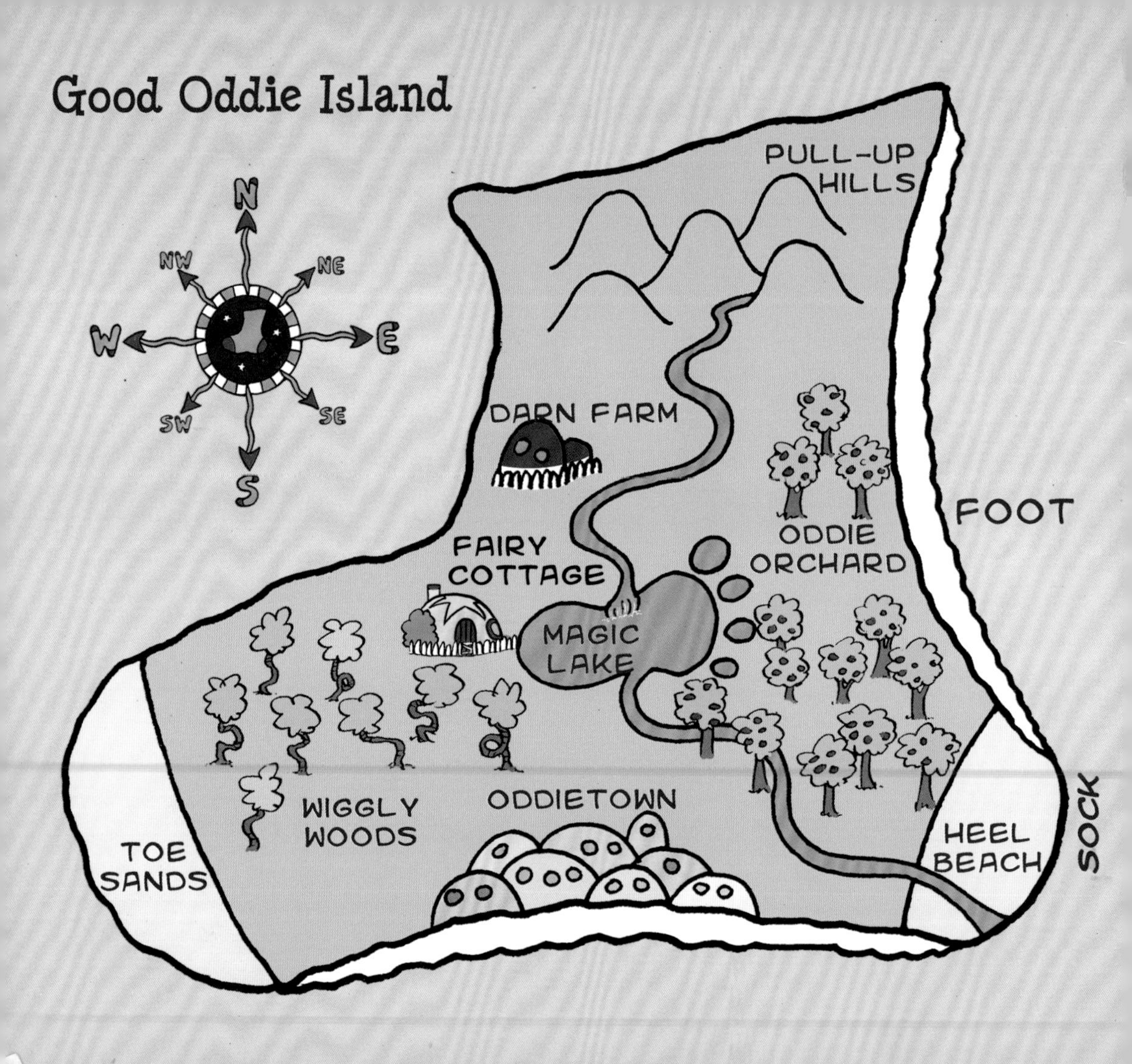
Good Oddie Island
N
NE
E
SE
S
SW
W
NW
PULL-UP HILLS
DARN FARM
FAIRY COTTAGE
MAGIC LAKE
ODDIE ORCHARD
FOOT
WIGGLY WOODS
ODDIETOWN
TOE SANDS
HEEL BEACH
SOCK